DISCARDED

English language consultant: Peter Viney

Contents

You can listen to the story online here:
usborneenglishreaders.com/
stonesoup

A man is walking on a quiet road. He is wearing an old coat and dirty old shoes. He is smiling, and sometimes he sings a song.

He walks all day.

At the end of the day, the man is
tired and hungry. He sees a house
near the road. He knocks on the door.
A woman opens the door.

Hello? What
do you want?

"Hello," says the man. "I'm very hungry. Do you have any food, please?"

"Sorry, but I don't know you," the woman answers.

I don't have any food for you.

"Oh, but I can show you something wonderful," says the man. "I can make soup from a stone!"

"How can you do that?" asks the woman.

"Can I come in?" asks the man.

My name is Harry.

"No, you can't come into my house," says the woman.

"Well, then, I can show you out here," says Harry. "I just need to make a fire. Can I take some wood, please? You have lots."

Harry makes a small fire. The woman doesn't know what to say.

"Now, I need a pot and some water," Harry says.

The woman brings him some water in a big pot. Harry puts the stone in it, then puts the pot on the fire. Soon the water is hot. Harry tastes it.

"It's good," he says, "but do you have any salt?"

"For the soup?" the woman asks.

"For the soup. It's better with salt."
The woman gives him some salt, and
he puts it in the pot.

He tastes it again. "It's good," he
says, "but do you have an onion?"

"For the soup, again?" The woman gives him an onion. Harry cuts it in pieces and puts it in the pot.

Oh yes, that's better.

"Hmm." Now Harry is thinking. "Do you have any potatoes?" he asks. The woman gives him some potatoes. He cuts them in pieces and puts them in the pot.

Soon he tastes the soup again. "Not bad," he says. "Some herbs? What do you think?"

The woman tastes the soup. "Some herbs, yes."

I have lots of herbs.

I have some cream, too.

She puts the herbs and the cream in
the pot, and they taste the soup again.
"That's really good!" says the woman.
"It is," says Harry.

I think
we can eat
it now.

"Let's have some bread with it. Oh,
and my name is Nell," says the woman.

Nell brings the bread outside.
She brings two bowls and
two spoons.

Nell and Harry sit down and eat all
the soup and the bread. Harry talks a
lot. He is kind and funny. Nell laughs.

"Wait, don't eat the stone!"
says Harry.

"Do you need it?" asks Nell.

"No, you can have it," says Harry.
"I can find another magic stone,
and you can make more soup. Just
don't forget…"

"…the salt," says Nell,

"Or the cream," says Nell. "Now
I can make soup from a stone, too.
What a wonderful evening!"

All kinds of soup

There are lots of different kinds of soup in the world.

You can make soup
with chicken...

...or with fish...

...or just with
vegetables.

Most soup is hot, but you
can have cold soup, too.

Do you like soup? Do people make a special kind
of soup in your home town or your country?

Activities

The answers are on page 24.

Can you see all these things in the picture?

Which three things *can't* you see?

tree   house   pot   bowl

bread   road   shoe   soup

table   dog   cat   coat

Harry's questions

Choose the right words.

1.

2.

3.

4.

Can I take some wood, please?

Do you have any salt?

Can I come in?

Do you have any food, please?

What is Harry doing?

Choose the right word for each sentence.

cutting   putting   tasting   walking

1.

A man is ....
on a quiet road.

2.

He is ....
the soup.

3.

Now he is ....
salt in the soup.

4.

He is ....
the potatoes in pieces.

What do you need?

Put the words in the right places.

| bowls   cream   herbs   an onion   potatoes |
| salt   spoons   some water   wood |

1.

You need .... to make a fire.

2.

You need ...., ..., ..., ..., ... and .... to make Harry's soup.

3.

You need .... and .... to eat soup.

What is Nell thinking?

Choose the right words.

That tastes nice.

Don't ask me for anything!

What is he doing?

What a wonderful evening!

1.

2.

3.

4.

Word list

bowl (n) you eat food like soup or rice from bowls.

cream (n) cream comes from milk. It has a nice, rich taste.

fire (n) you use fire to make things hot and to cook things.

herb (n) a green plant with a strong taste. You use herbs for cooking.

knock (v) when you want to go in to a place, you knock (make a sound with your hand) on the door.

onion (n) a vegetable that grows under the ground and has a strong taste.

piece (n) a small part of something. You often cut thing in pieces to cook them.

pot (n) you put food in a pot when you need to cook it.

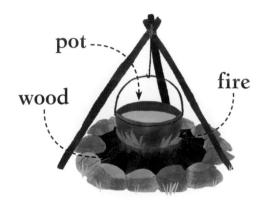

pot

wood

fire

potato (n) a vegetable that grows under the ground and is white inside.

salt (n) salt is white, and you put it on or in food to give it more taste.

soup (n) a kind of food that you can make with meat, fish or vegetables.

spoon (n) you use a spoon to eat food, especially liquid food like soup.

stone (n) a stone is hard and you find it on the ground.

taste (v) to try food and see if it is good.

wonderful (adj) when something is wonderful, it is really good.

wood (n) wood comes from trees. You can use wood to make a fire.

soup **bowl** **spoon**

Answers

Can you see all these things in the picture?
Three things you can't see: dog, house, road.

Harry's questions
1. Do you have any food, please?
2. Can I come in?
3. Can I take some wood, please?
4. Do you have any salt?

What is Harry doing?
1. walking
2. tasting
3. putting
4. cutting

What do you need?
1. wood
2. some water, salt, an onion, potatoes, herbs, cream.
3. bowls, spoons.

What is Nell thinking?
1. Don't ask me for anything!
2. What is he doing?
3. That tastes nice.
4. What a wonderful evening!

You can find information about other Usborne English Readers here: usborneenglishreaders.com

Designed by Jodie Smith
Edited by Jane Chisholm

First published in 2020 by Usborne Publishing Ltd.,
Usborne House, 83-85 Saffron Hill, London EC1N 8RT, England.
usborne.com Copyright © 2020 Usborne Publishing Ltd.